W9-CBT-337

Weaving, fishing, and storytelling are all
part of this spirited book that celebrates
Native American traditions as it teaches young
children to count from one to ten. Each number introduces a facet of Native American
culture, while the simple rhyming text is enhanced by a brief afterword on Native
American customs. Ideal for storytime or bedtime, this is a book sure to leave
children counting rabbits instead of sheep.

"Hurray! At long last primary school educators and lovers of children's
literature have an accurate American Indian book written for primary
children."
—*The Five Owls*

". . . teachers looking for picture books that cut across the curriculum
will find this a good way to combine a unit on Native Americans with
counting . . ."
—*Booklist*

". . . guaranteed to pique interest in counting for youngest children,
and in Native American cultures for older ones."
—*Los Angeles Times*

"Informative pictures invite group sharing, while the gentle mood
suits bedtime . . ."
—*School Library Journal*

"A hit for children. . . . Teachers will love this one, too."
—*American Bookseller, "Pick of the Lists"*

WINNER OF THE INTERNATIONAL READING ASSOCIATION CHILDREN'S BOOK AWARD

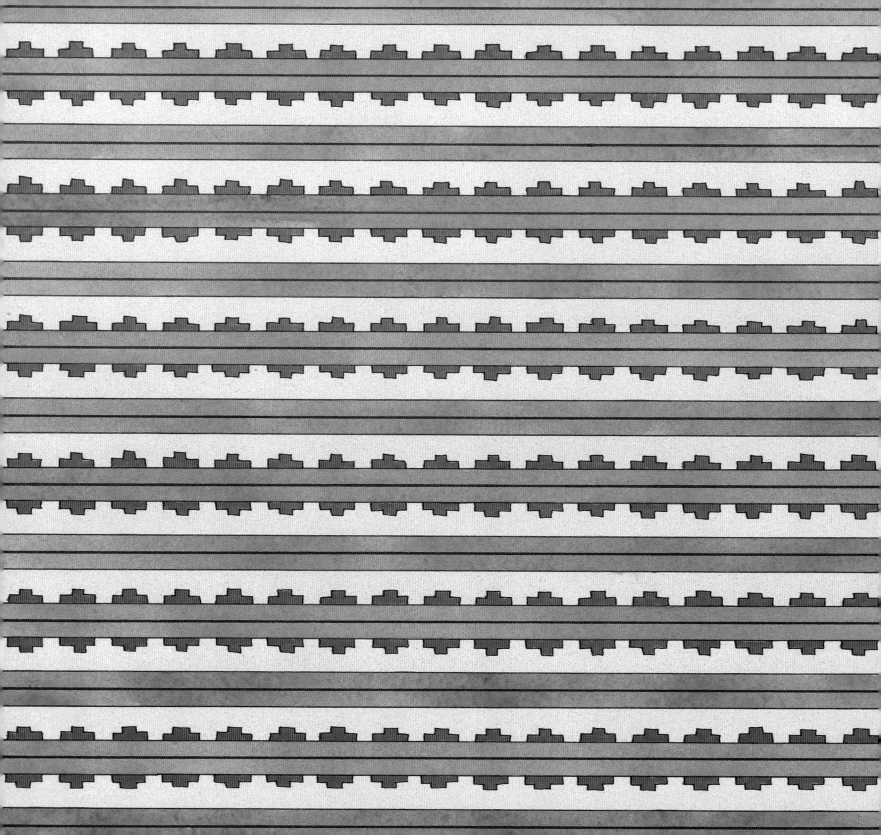

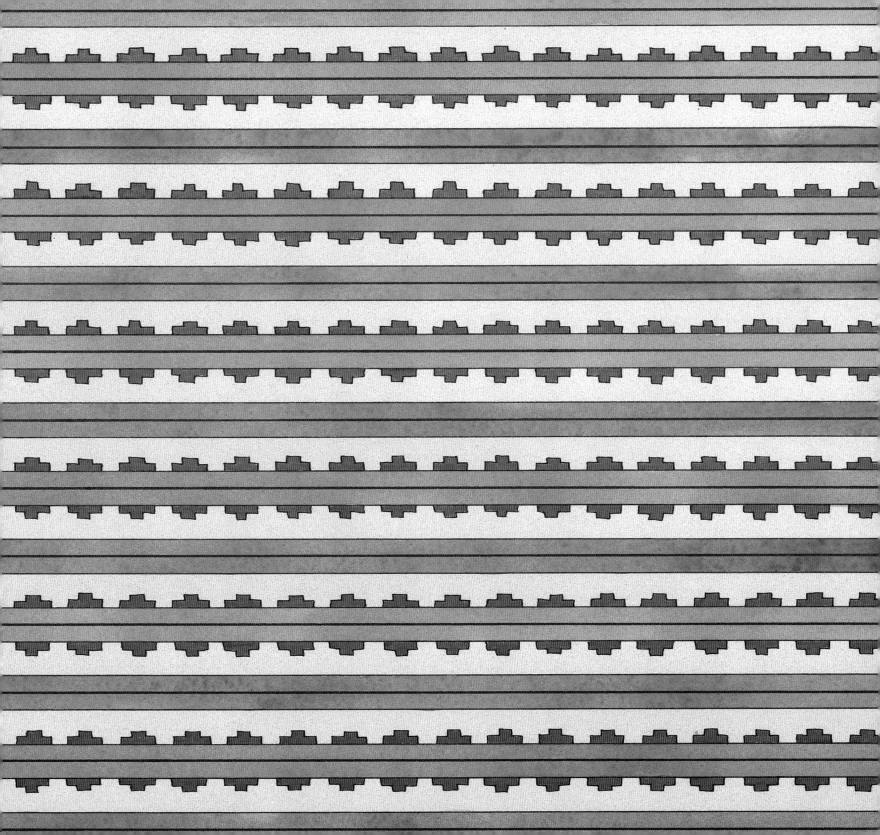

Text © 1991 by Virginia Grossman.
Illustrations © 1991 by Sylvia Long.
All rights reserved.
Book design by Julie Noyes.
Manufactured in Hong Kong.

For Andrew, Emily, Gretchen, John, and Matthew

Grossman, Virginia.
    Ten little rabbits / by Virginia Grossman ; illustrated by Sylvia Long.
    32p.   24.7 x 22.2cm.
    Summary: A counting rhyme with illustrations of rabbits in Native American
costume, depicting traditional customs such as rain dances, hunting, and smoke signals. Includes a glossary with additional information on the customs.
    ISBN 0-8118-1057-7 (pb.)
    ISBN 0-87701-552-X (hc.)
    1. Indians of North America—Social life and customs—Juvenile literature. 2.
Counting-out rhymes—Juvenile literature. [1. Indians of North America—Social life
and customs. 2. Counting.] I. Long, Sylvia, ill. II. Title.
    E98.S7G87 1991
    394'.08997—dc20
    [E]   90-2011
                                                               CIP
                                                               AC

Distributed in Canada by Raincoast Books
9050 Shaughnessy Street, Vancouver, British Columbia V6P 6E5

10 9 8

Chronicle Books LLC
85 Second Street
San Francisco, California 94105

www.chroniclekids.com

TEN LITTLE RABBITS

by Virginia Grossman

illustrated by Sylvia Long

chronicle books · san francisco

One lonely traveler riding on the plain.

Two graceful dancers asking for some rain.

Three busy messengers sending out the news.

Four clever trackers looking for some clues.

Five wise storytellers trying to keep warm.

Six nimble runners fleeing from a storm.

Seven merry mischief-makers playing hide-and-seek.

Eight patient anglers fishing in a creek.

Nine festive drummers beating on a drum.

Ten sleepy weavers knowing day is done.

SIOUX

1 The Plains tribes depended on buffalo for food, clothing, bedding, and housing materials. They followed the herds, moving camp when the buffalo moved to new grazing areas. Prior to acquiring the horse, these tribes used dog travois to carry wood, food, small children, and the elderly. Although the child in this illustration is pictured alone, she would actually be part of a large group traveling together.

TEWA

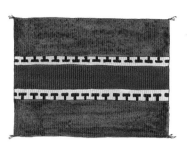

2 Traditionally, all Rio Grande pueblos stage a corn dance, generally in the Spring. The dancers wear crimson parrot feathers and cowrie shells from the Pacific and carry gourd rattles. The male dancers leap and stamp to wake up the spirits. Finally, their evergreen finery (symbolic of the fir tree that, according to legend, people used to climb up from the underworld) is thrown in the river in the hope of pleasing the *Shiwana*, the rain-cloud people.

UTE

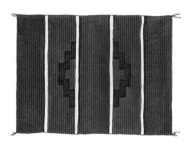

3 Plains tribes used smoke signals as a method of long-distance communication. Using a system of short and long puffs, they sent messages about such things as the presence of buffalo or the approach of enemies.

MENOMINEE

4 In the Great Lakes region, hunting bear had both practical and symbolic importance. Its fur was used for warmth, its flesh for food, and its fat was used as cooking oil, medicinal salves, and insect repellent. Its claws often made prize ornaments.

BLACKFOOT

5 Storytellers have always been a respected part of traditional Native American culture. They carried with them the legends, myths, and personal history of the tribe. In the oral tradition, this history had to be passed from one generation to the other by word of mouth.

HOPI

6 The Hopi lived on the tops of mesas in Southwestern areas that had no permanent watercourses. Because of this, they farmed in the desert below where the success of their crops was dependent on rainfall and flash floods.

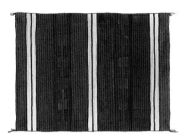

ARAPAHO

7 Because tribes often had to be mobile in order to survive, it was essential that possessions be kept to a minimum. It seems likely, toys and games were not considered a necessity, and so children had to rely on simple games to entertain themselves. Though there is no actual documentation of children playing hide-and-seek, it is possible that such a universal game was indeed played by children, both for entertainment and as a way to improve tracking skills.

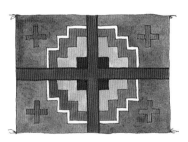

NEZ PERCE

8 Tribes in the Northwest had no agricultural tradition until the missionaries came. Salmon was a staple food and noted fishing holes were considered the common property of the tribe. They supplemented salmon with trout, sturgeon, deer, elk, and small game.

KWAKIUTL

9 The Northwest Coastal tribes carved decorations on wooden drums, boxes, house posts, partition screens, etc. The masks and costumes in this illustration are from the Kwakiutl tribe.

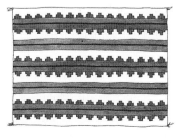

NAVAJO

10 For centuries, Navajo weavers have made beautiful rugs and blankets, both for their own use and for trade. It is said that the traditional patterns simply emerge from the weaver's memories and that there is always a break within the pattern so that the maker's spirit can escape. All of the blankets on these pages represent some of the many designs traditionally woven by Navajo weavers. They can be seen on the cover of this book as well.

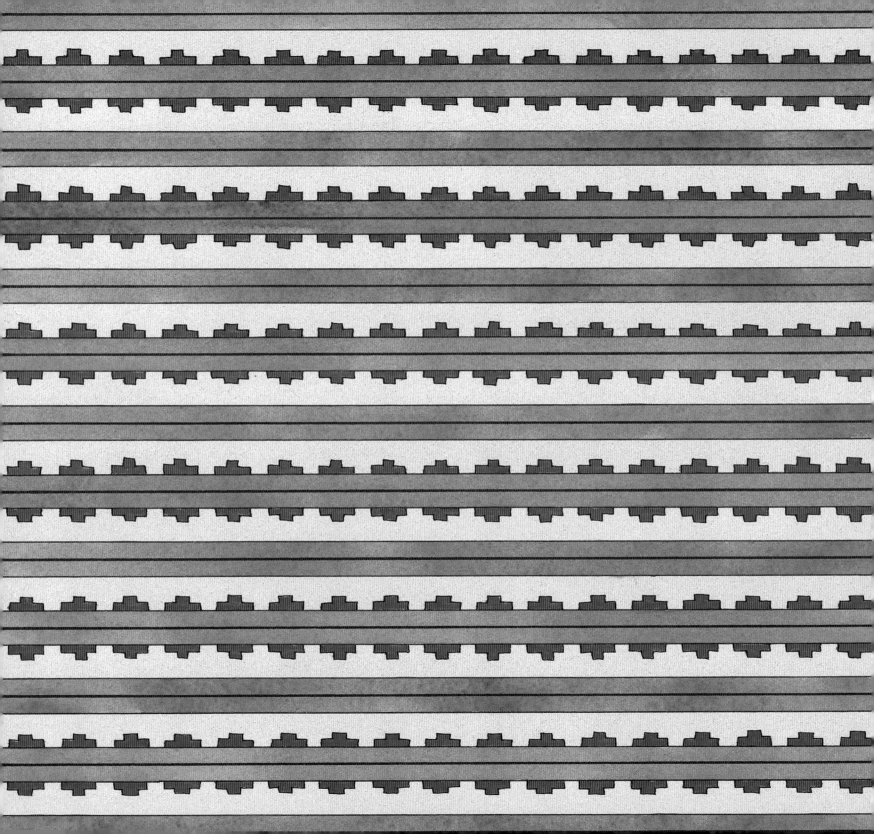

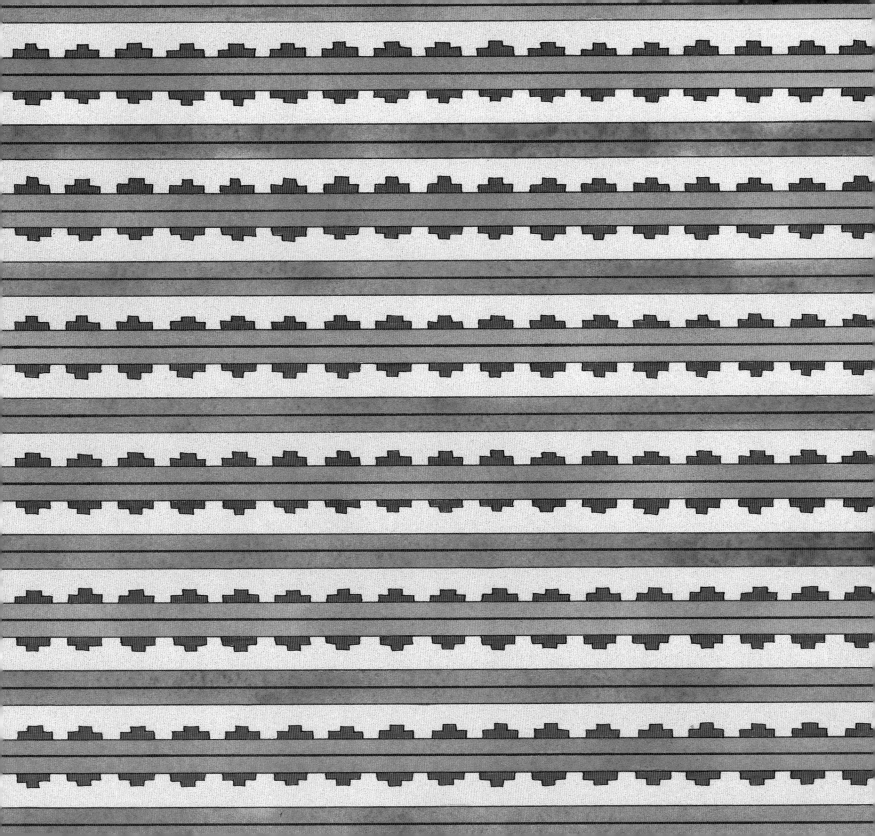

SYLVIA LONG first became fascinated with Native American cultures as she listened to her grandfather's stories about his youth spent working on a reservation. Years later, Ms. Long herself lived on a reservation in Wyoming, while her husband, a physician, worked for the Indian Health Service. This experience, combined with a reading of *Watership Down*, inspired a series of Native American rabbit illustrations that later became the basis for this book.

Ms. Long graduated from the Maryland Institute of Art and has exhibited extensively for the past twenty years. She lives in Arizona with her husband and their sons, Matthew and John.

VIRGINIA GROSSMAN was born and raised in a small town in Iowa. She completed her undergraduate and graduate degrees in Engineering at Brown University and now lives in Washington with her husband and their three children, Andrew, Emily, and Gretchen. This is her first children's book.

ALSO ILLUSTRATED BY SYLVIA LONG

Alejandro's Gift by Richard E. Albert
Deck the Hall by Silvia Long
Fire Race by Jonathan London
Hush Little Baby by Sylvia Long
Liplap's Wish by Jonathan London
Sylvia Long's Mother Goose
Sylvia Long's Mother Goose Nesting Blocks
Twinkle, Twinkle, Little, Star by Sylvia Long